P9-DOE-554

FRIENDSHIP TALES

DISNEY PRESS

Los Angeles • New York

CONTENTS

Mickey's Perfecto Day!, First Edition, October 2017
Donald's Stinky Day, First Edition, June 2020
Minnie-rella, First Edition, December 2013
A Hot-Dog Day, First Edition, June 2007
First Bind-Up Edition, July 2020
1 3 5 7 9 10 8 6 4 2
ISBN 978-1-368-05542-0
FAC-029261-20150
Library of Congress Catalog Number: 2020933712
Printed in the United States of America
For more Disney Press fun, visit www.disneybooks.com

SUSTAINABLE FORESTRY INITIATIVE
Certified Sourcing
www.sfiprogram.org
SFI-01415

Disney Junior

MICKEY MOUSE ROADSTER RACERS

MICKEY'S PERFECTO DAY!

Adapted by

Sherri Stoner

Based on the episode written by

Ashley Mendoza

Illustrated by

Loter, Inc.

Mickey and his pals pack for a trip.
They are going to Madrid, Spain.
They will see the sights.
Donald will sing with his friends.
It will be a *perfecto* day!

The gang drives their Daily
Drivers to Madrid.

They pass a baby bull sniffing a rose.
The rose falls off the bush.
It lands in Minnie's car!

Minnie puts the rose behind her ear.
The baby bull runs after his rose.
Minnie does not notice.

The gang gets to Spain.
Mickey and Minnie go to the market.
It is a *perfecto* day!
The baby bull follows his nose to
the rose.

Minnie shops.

Minnie tries on dresses.

The baby bull sniffs the rose.

Minnie does not notice.

But Mickey notices!
"B-b-b-bull!" Mickey shouts.

Mickey and Minnie jump into a cart.
It rolls away from the bull.
It rolls into . . .

. . . a churro cart!

"We will take two," says Mickey.

Donald finds his friends.
They invite Daisy and Donald to lunch.
It is a *perfecto* day!

Donald tries the potatoes.

"AAAACK!" he shouts.

They are very spicy.

Daisy tries to help.
She gives him water to drink.

It is almost time to sing.
The group warms up.
Donald opens his mouth.
No sound comes out.

Who will sing at the show?
Donald's friends ask Daisy to sing!

Donald is sad he cannot sing
with his friends.
He gives Daisy his hat.

Poor Donald.
His friend brings him dessert.
He will watch the show from his
table.

Mickey and Minnie visit the plaza.
The bull visits the plaza, too.

He follows his nose to the rose.
Mickey and Minnie run!

The friends find a spot to
hide in.
The baby bull runs right
by them.

Mickey and Minnie run to the show.
Daisy is singing with the band.

Donald finishes dessert.
He gets the bill.
"WHAT?" he shouts.
His voice is back!

Donald joins the band.

They sing together.

The crowd loves the show!

The baby bull comes to the show, too.
He sits next to Minnie.
He sniffs her rose.

"He just likes my flower!" Minnie
says.
She gives the bull her rose.
The bull gives Mickey a kiss!

Minnie giggles.
What a *perfecto* day!

SKI TRIPPIN'

Adapted by
Sheila Sweeny Higginson

Based on the episode written by
Mike Kubat

Illustrated by
Loter, Inc.

Mickey and his friends are going skiing.

Daisy packs up the van. "Did I forget something?" she asks herself.

They drive up, up, up into the
mountains.

Daisy unpacks her skis and poles.

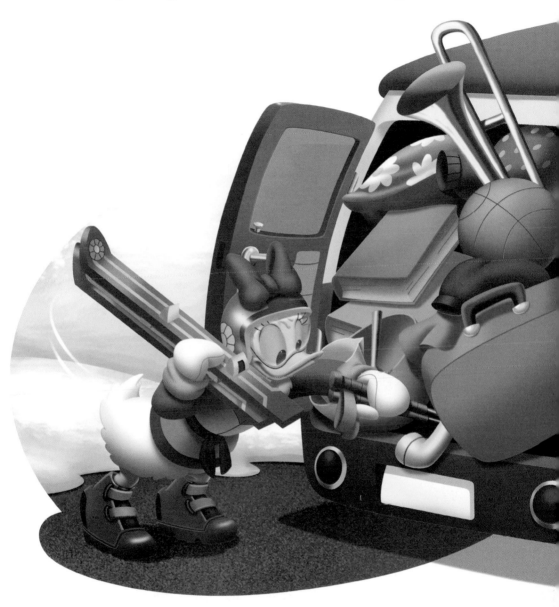

Daisy swings her skis around and around.

"Wak!"
says Donald.

"Sorry!"
says Daisy.

Daisy puts her skis on backward!

She slips and slides on the snow.

"I forgot to learn how to ski!"
Daisy cries.

Daisy crashes into a pile of snow.
Donald comes to help her.

"Maybe I should go home,"
says Daisy.
"No way!" says Minnie.
"We can teach you to ski,"
says Mickey.

"First we get on the ski lift,"
says Mickey.
"I think I have the hang of it!"
says Daisy.

Mickey has a trick called the Sly
Stepper.
Lean low, and around you go!
"Now you try," Mickey says to Daisy.

Daisy starts skiing down the hill.
"Lean low, and around I—
WHOA!" she says.

Goofy has a trick called the Patented
Plow.
It will help Daisy slow down.
"Make a V with your skis," Goofy
says to Daisy.
Daisy makes a V. It turns into an X!
She trips and falls.

Donald has a trick called the Tail
Feather Tuck.
"Tuck in, tail up, and go!" Donald
says to Daisy.
"Now you try."

Daisy skis down the hill.
Faster, faster, faster!

Oh, no! Daisy crashes into Donald.
"I quit," says Daisy.
But Minnie will not let her give up!

Minnie has a trick called the
Mogulizer.
Left pole, turn. Right pole, turn.
She skis around the bumps.
Daisy can do it, too!

Here comes Pete.
He is late for the big ski race.
It is starting in **3** . . . **2** . . . **1** . . .

Pete pushes Daisy.
She hits the rope tow.
It sends her flying!

Minnie skis after Daisy.
Mickey skis after Minnie.
Donald skis after Mickey.
Goofy skis after Donald.

Daisy lands in the middle of
the race!

FROZEN MOOSE
FREESTYLE CLASSIC

"Daisy is in the lead!" says the
announcer.

Daisy uses the tricks she learned
from her friends.

She wins the race!

Does Daisy want to celebrate with
some hot cocoa?

No, she wants to keep skiing.
"Ski you later!" she says to her
friends.

DISNEY Junior

MICKEY MOUSE ROADSTER RACERS

DONALD'S STINKY DAY

Adapted by
Bill Scollon

Based on the episode written by
Mike Kubat

Illustrated by
Loter, Inc.

Donald packs a picnic lunch.
A seagull steals his hot dog!
He reaches for it . . .

. . . and falls in the water!
Daisy calls Donald.
"I need your help in the park,"
she says.

Donald drives to the park.
He sees a dog barking at
something in a tree.

"Don't worry, kitty," says Donald.
"I will help you."

Donald points to his hat.

"Hop on!" he says.

The animal in the tree is not a cat.

Donald saved a skunk!

"Pee-yew!" says Daisy.
"You need a bath."

Donald drives to Mickey's Garage.
The skunk follows him.

Donald wants to work on his roadster.

The skunk tries to help him.

Uh-oh! She drops the wrench.

"YEOW!" shouts Donald.

"What an odd choice for a pet,"
says Mickey.
"She is not my pet!" says Donald.

Donald's friends send him through
the Auto Wash.
He gets sprayed with soapy water.
Brushes scrub away the skunk smell.

Goofy and Donald go out for hot dogs.
"All it needs is ketchup," says Donald.
Look who came to help her best
buddy!

Donald grabs the bottle.
He squeezes too hard. *SPLAT!*
"I am out of here!" Donald yells.

Mickey and Donald go fishing.
"I made this a No Skunks zone,"
Donald says.

The skunk followed them!
When she jumps into the lake,
the fish jump into the boat.

When she jumps back into the boat,
the fish jump back into the lake.

"She wants to be your friend,"
Mickey tells Donald.
But Donald has a plan to get rid
of the skunk.

Donald takes the skunk to the park
for a picnic.
"Oh, no! I forgot the potato chips,"
says Donald. "Be right back!"

But Donald drives away for good.
"Bye-bye, stinker!" he yells.

Donald hits a nest of bees.
They chase after him.
"What do they want?" Donald yells.

Donald ZOOMS and ZIGZAGS
all the way to Mickey's Garage.

The bees keep chasing him.

Everyone hides when they see the angry swarm of bees.

Everyone except the skunk!
She sprays the bees.
The bees buzz off!

"You saved me!" says Donald.

"What a good friend," says Minnie.
"Friends," says Donald.
"Yeah, we ARE friends!"

Donald takes his new friend
to the park.
They help Daisy plant flowers.
Daisy helps the skunk, too!
"BEE-utiful!" says Donald.

Adapted by
Lisa Ann Marsoli

Based on the episode written by
Ashley Mendoza

Illustrated by
Loter, Inc.

Mickey wants to surprise Minnie.
He needs to keep Minnie busy.
"Can you take care of my frog?"
Goofy asks.

"And sweep the floor?" Daisy adds.
"And wash my rubber duckies?"
says Donald.

"I have a lot to do," says Minnie. First she washes the rubber duckies.

Next she fixes Pluto's bear.
"I am so tired," says Minnie.
Soon she is asleep!

"Minnie-rella!" a voice calls.
"I am your fairy godmother!
It is time to get ready for Prince
Mickey's ball!"
Minnie-rella has too much to do.

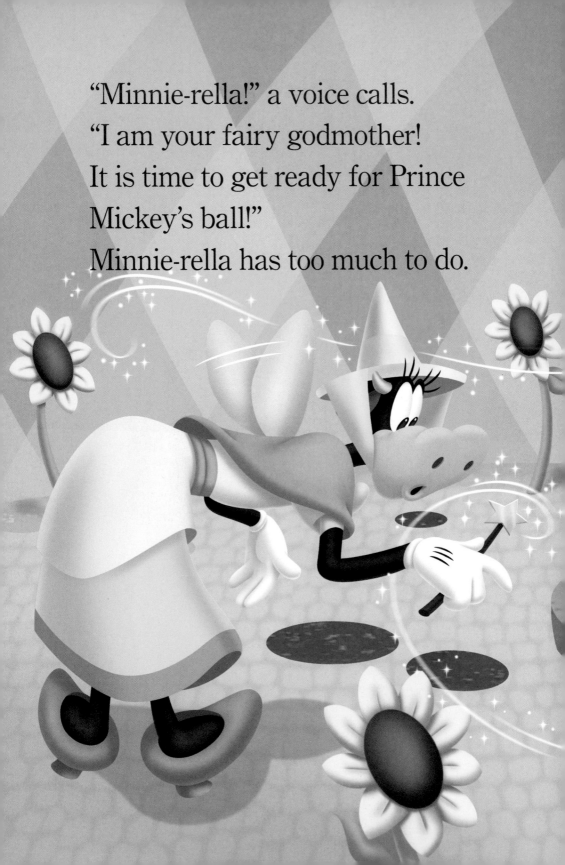

The Fairy Godmother will help.
She waves her wand.
Oops! Flowers grow out of the floor!
"Oh, Quoodles," the Fairy
Godmother calls.

Quoodles brings a pillow, a hippo,
a ribbon, and the mystery tool.
They will save the tools for later.

The Handy Helpers help clean.
"Now you can go to Prince Mickey's
ball," the Fairy Godmother says.

"I need a dress," says Minnie-rella.
"Here," the Fairy Godmother says.
Oh, no! The dress is in pieces!
"Oops!" says the Fairy Godmother.

The Fairy Godmother whistles.
Some little friends come to help.
Soon Minnie-rella has a lovely dress.

Now Minnie-rella needs a new bow.
"Hmmm," says the Fairy Godmother.
"Which tool can we use?"
"The ribbon!" says Minnie-rella.

The Fairy Godmother looks down.
"Your shoes will not do at all!"
she cries.

She waves her
wand once.

"Oops!"

She tries again.

"Oops!"

"Once more," says
the Fairy Godmother.

"That is it!"

"You are ready!" says the Fairy
Godmother.

"How will I get there?" asks
Minnie-rella.

They go to Goofy's garden.

The Fairy Godmother asks for a
pumpkin.
"I do not have any pumpkins,"
Goofy says. "But I have a big
tomato."

The tomato turns into a carriage.
Goofy turns into a coachman!
"Be home before midnight!"
says the Fairy Godmother.

On the way to the ball, the
carriage gets stuck in a hole!
Minnie-rella calls Quoodles.
Which tool can help?

Maybe the hippo can push the
carriage out of the hole!
The hippo taps the carriage.
Away it goes!

Soon Minnie-rella and Goofy
come to the castle gate.
"It takes three diamonds to
unlock the gate," Pete says.

Quoodles brings the mystery tool.
It is a bracelet with three diamonds.
The three diamonds unlock the gate.
Minnie-rella can go to the ball!

Minnie-rella runs to the ball.
She dances with Prince Mickey.
Prince Mickey has found his
princess!

Soon it is midnight.

"I have to go!" cries Minnie-rella.

"Wait! I do not know your name,"
Prince Mickey calls.

"How will I find her?" he asks.
Pluto sees the glass slipper.
Prince Mickey must find the one
who fits the glass slipper.

Prince Mickey begins his search.
Goofy tries on the glass slipper.
It does not fit.

The slipper is going to break!
Quoodles brings the pillow.
Prince Mickey catches the slipper!

Goofy takes Prince Mickey to see
Minnie-rella.
The glass slipper fits!

The prince and princess will live
happily ever after!

"Wake up, Minnie!" call her friends.
Mickey gives her a present.
"I dreamed of shoes like these!"
Minnie says. "Thank you!"

"You look like a princess,"
says Mickey.
"You will always be my prince!"
Minnie says.

The friends do the Hot Dog
Dance. Minnie loves her new
glass slippers. She does the
best dance of all!

A HOT-DOG DAY

Things for Picnic:
Tablecloth
Napkins
Plates
Fruit Salad
Lemonade
Corn on the Cob
Hot Dogs
Buns
Ketchup
Mustard

Written by
Sheila Sweeny Higginson

Illustrated by the
Disney Storybook Artists

Minnie is planning a picnic for
her friends.
She makes a shopping list.
She makes invitations.

Minnie gets the picnic basket.
She puts a tablecloth, napkins,
and plates inside.

Minnie picks flowers for the
picnic table.
"These need a vase," she says.
She goes to look for one.
She leaves the picnic basket in
the garden.

Daisy finds the picnic basket.
"Minnie is planning a picnic?"
she says.
"I love picnics!"

"I will bring fruit salad,"
says Daisy.

A minute later, Minnie comes looking for the picnic basket. But it is not in the garden.

Daisy has the picnic basket.
She picks blueberries for the
fruit salad.

"I need a big bowl," says Daisy.
She leaves the picnic basket by
the blueberry bush.

Daisy adds watermelon to the
fruit salad.

She adds pineapple, too.

Donald finds the picnic basket.

"Finally, someone is planning
a picnic," he says.
"I will bring lemonade."

A minute later, Daisy comes
looking for the picnic basket.
But it is not by the blueberry
bush.

Donald has the picnic basket.
He goes to the store for lemons
and sugar.

Careful, Donald! The stack of
lemons falls apart.
Donald leaves the picnic basket in
the store.

Goofy finds the picnic basket.
"Oh, boy! A picnic!" he says.
"I will bring corn on the cob."

A minute later, Donald comes
looking for the picnic basket.
But it is not in the store.

Goofy has the picnic basket.
He goes to the cornfield.

Goofy gets lots of corn!
He leaves the picnic basket at the
cornfield.

Goofy sings a corny song:
"Corn, corn, wonderful corn!
Cornflakes, corn bread, corn
dogs, too. Corn on the cob for me
and you!"

Mickey finds the picnic basket.
"Minnie is having a picnic,"
Mickey says to Pluto. "I will get
the last things on her list."

Mickey goes to the store.
He buys hot dogs, buns, ketchup,
and mustard.

"We better hurry!" says Mickey.

Everyone arrives right on time.
They have everything from
Minnie's list.

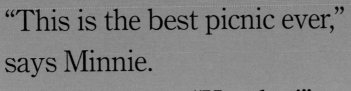

"This is the best picnic ever,"
says Minnie.
Mickey agrees. "Hot dog!"

THE END